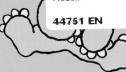

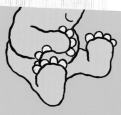

For Eve & Alice K.C.
For Mum & Dad S.H.

Text © 1999 Kathryn Cave
Illustrations © 1999 Sue Hendra

Original edition published under the title
Henry's Song
By Lion Publishing plc, Oxford, England
© 1999 Lion Publishing

This edition published 2000
under license from Lion Publishing by
Eerdmans Books for Young Readers
An imprint of Wm. B. Eerdmans Publishing Company
255 Jefferson Ave., S.E., Grand Rapids, Michigan 49503 /
P.O. Box 163, Cambridge CB3 9PU U.K.

Printed and bound in Singapore

05 04 03 02 01 00   7 6 5 4 3 2 1

Library of Congress Cataloging-in-Publication Data

Cave, Kathryn
Henry's Song / written by Kathryn Cave: illustrated by Sue Hendra.
p.   cm.
Summary: The animals try to please the maker of all things
by singing for him, but they do not want Henry to join them
in their song because they do not like the way he sounds.
ISBN 0-8028-5198-3 (cl. : alk. paper)
[1.Singing Fiction. 2. Animals Fiction. 3. Individuality Fiction.]
I. Hendra, Sue, ill. II. Title.
PZ7.C29114Hg   2000
[E] – dc21   99-37942
                          CIP

Typeset in 17/32 Stone Informal

Henry's Song

Written by Kathryn Cave
Illustrated by Sue Hendra

Eerdmans Books for Young Readers

Grand Rapids, Michigan / Cambridge, U.K.

Early one morning, while the forest was still asleep,
Henry woke up. The sun had just risen.

The grass shone with dew.

It was a beautiful day to be alive.

Henry felt happy.

He did something he had never done before.

He took a deep breath and he sang.

The song was loud, and joyful, and full of surprises.

All at once, the forest woke up.

"What's that noise?" the creatures cried.

"Put a sock in it, Henry!"

Henry didn't hear them.

Soon there was snarling and shrieking,

shouting and cheeping,

trumpeting, cawing, growling, and

roaring all over the forest.

Suddenly, the bright sky grew dark.

"What's all this noise?" asked a voice like thunder.

It was the Maker of All Things.

The trees shook, the grass trembled,

and everyone became very quiet.

"Listen to me," said the voice. "I made you, and I made you
well. I gave you legs to run, paws to dig, eyes to find food,
and mouths to eat it. I gave you ears so that you can hear me.
Now tell me this: what are your voices for?"

None of the creatures said a word. Nobody knew the answer.

"Think about it," said the voice. "Tomorrow I will ask again."

The grass shook, the trees trembled, and the Maker
of All Things left the forest.

All morning the creatures argued about

how to answer the Maker's question.

Their voices were all so different.

Some croaked. Some cawed. Some cooed. Some roared.

There was not one noise they could all make together.

What were their voices for?

At last someone said, "This morning Henry's song put the
Maker in a bad mood. Tomorrow let's sing a proper song,
the most beautiful song the forest has ever heard.
Then the Maker will be pleased, and there will be
no more questions."
Everyone stopped arguing and shouted, "Yes!"

The creatures wanted their song to be perfect,
so they practiced. They squashed and squeezed
themselves into a circle.

One by one they made their way to the center
of the circle and lifted their own special voices.
When Henry's turn came, he clasped his paws,
he lifted his head, and he sang with all his heart.

Henry's song was very special.

The others might have liked it if they had listened properly,

but they hadn't. They covered their ears and said, "Call that

singing? We'll never please the Maker with a noise like that!"

Then they said Henry couldn't join in their song for the Maker.

He begged and pleaded, but they went on saying "No!"

until the forest went to sleep.

The next morning the creatures sang for the Maker of All Things.

It was a wonderful song, but something was missing.

The Maker of All Things knew what it was.

"Stop!" said the voice like thunder.

"Why can't I hear Henry?"

"I can't sing," said Henry, hanging his head.

"Can't sing? But of course you can!

That's what voices are for!" cried the Maker.

"To make your song perfect, you need to sing together.

Would you try that?" asked the Maker gently.

"All of you? Every single one?"

So the creatures did.

'Lift your hearts, your hands, your voices!

Please the Maker with your noises!

Happy hearts and voices bring.

This song's for everyone to sing!"

"That's perfect!" said
the Maker of All Things.
And it was.